The Graphic Shakespeare Series

Twelfth Night

Retold by Hilary Burningham
Illustrated by Neil Deans

Evans Brothers Limited

THE CHARACTERS IN THE PLAY

Viola	– a shipwrecked lady, later disguised as Cesario
Duke Orsino	– Duke of Illyria, in love with Lady Olivia
Lady Olivia	– a rich countess
Sebastian	– also shipwrecked, twin brother of Viola
Malvolio	– Olivia's steward, managed her household
Feste	– Olivia's jester
Maria	– Olivia's attendant, her lady-in-waiting
Sir Toby Belch	– Olivia's uncle
Sir Andrew Aguecheek	– friend of Sir Toby
Fabian	– a member of Olivia's household
The Captain	– Captain of the wrecked ship
Antonio	– another sea-captain, friend of Sebastian
Valentine	– Orsino's servant, his messenger to Lady Olivia
The Priest	– Olivia's priest
Curio	– another servant to Orsino

PORTRAIT GALLERY

Viola

Duke Orsino

Lady Olivia

Sebastian

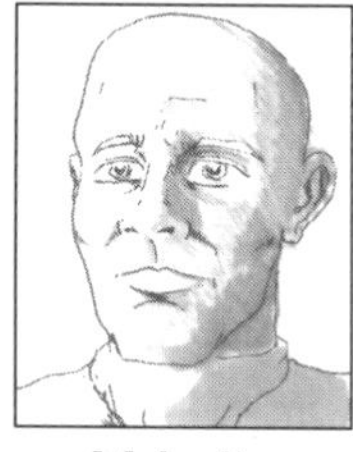
Malvolio

Feste

Maria

Sir Toby Belch

Sir Andrew Aguecheek

Fabian

The Captain

Antonio

Valentine

The Priest

ACT ONE

Orsino, Duke of Illyria, was listening to music. He was thinking about Olivia, the lady he loved. At first, the music seemed beautiful to him, but suddenly he was tired of it.

Orsino's servant, Valentine, had tried to see Lady Olivia. She refused to see him. Her brother was dead, and she had decided to shut herself away for seven years. Every day, she cried for her brother.

Orsino felt hopeful anyway. One day, Olivia might love him even more than she had loved her brother. He would continue to dream of her.

ORSINO: Away before me to sweet beds of flowers!
Love thoughts lie rich when canopied with bowers.

In another part of Illyria, there had been a shipwreck. Viola was saved, but she was very sad. She thought that her brother was drowned. The captain of the wrecked ship told her that he had seen her brother tie himself to a mast[1]. Her brother and the mast floated away on the waves. Perhaps he had not drowned.

The captain was from Illyria. He told Viola all about it. Orsino, the Duke, ruled Illyria. Everyone knew that the Duke was in love with Lady Olivia. One year before, Olivia's father had died, and after that, her brother. Olivia was very sad. She had loved them both. Now, she wanted to stay at home alone. Most of all, she did not want to see other men.

[1]mast – a long pole or piece of wood that holds up the sails of a sailing ship

VIOLA: Knowest thou this country?
CAPTAIN: Ay, madam, well, for I was bred and born
Not three hours' travel from this very place.

The captain was a good man. Viola knew that she could trust him.

She had a plan. She asked him to take her to Orsino. She wanted to be Orsino's servant. To do this, she would have to dress as a young man.

She needed a disguise[1]. She would pay the captain well if he helped her dress as a young man.

Only the captain would know who she really was. He promised not to tell anyone.

[1]disguise – clothes or make-up to make someone look completely different

VIOLA: Conceal me what I am, and be my aid
For such disguise as haply shall become
The form of my intent. I'll serve this Duke.

At Lady Olivia's house, Maria, the housekeeper, was telling off Sir Toby Belch[1]. He was Lady Olivia's uncle. Olivia did not like Sir Toby getting drunk all the time. He came home late, and made a lot of noise. And she didn't like his friend, Sir Andrew Aguecheek, either.

Sir Toby hoped that the Lady Olivia would marry Sir Andrew Aguecheek. Maria thought there wasn't much chance of that.

[1]The word *belch* means the noise made by air coming up from the stomach through the throat.

MARIA: By my troth, Sir Toby, you must come in earlier o'nights. Your cousin, my lady, takes great exception to your ill hours.

Sir Andrew came to see Sir Toby. He was feeling unhappy. Olivia refused to see him, and anyway, Duke Orsino also wanted to marry her. Orsino was young, rich and handsome. Sir Andrew thought he might as well return to his own home.

Sir Toby tried to cheer him up. They had a drink together, then another.

They became more and more noisy. They shouted and danced. They were drunk. They didn't care.

SIR ANDREW: Shall we set about some revels?
SIR TOBY: What shall we do else? Were we not born under Taurus?
SIR ANDREW: Taurus? That's sides and heart.
SIR TOBY: No, sir, it is legs and thighs. Let me see thee caper. Ha! Higher! Ha! Ha! Excellent!

By now, Viola, dressed as a young man, was working for the Duke Orsino. She called herself Cesario. Already, the Duke liked her and trusted her.

Viola was to go to the Lady Olivia's house. She must somehow see the Lady Olivia. The Duke told her to be rude if necessary!

The Duke was starting to notice things about "Cesario". For example, Cesario had very red lips, his voice was high, and he had no beard. Would the Duke find out that Cesario was really a woman?

On her side, Viola was starting to fall in love with Orsino. As Cesario, she had to go and tell Olivia about his love. In fact, Viola wanted to be Orsino's wife.

ORSINO: Diana's lip
Is not more smooth and rubious; thy small pipe
Is as the maiden's organ, shrill and sound,
And all is semblative a woman's part.

Lady Olivia had a jester[1] named Feste. Feste tried to make her laugh. Lady Olivia was very sad. She didn't want to laugh. She told her servants to take Feste away.

He tried to show that she was foolish to feel so sad about her brother. If he was in heaven, she should feel happy.

Lady Olivia asked her steward[2], Malvolio, what he thought of Feste. Malvolio said he did not think Feste was funny. People were fools themselves if they laughed at Feste's jokes.

That was a cruel thing to say. Feste would remember it. In fact, he was a very good jester.

[1]jester – a person paid to make people laugh; a comedian
[2]steward – someone who was in charge of the household

MALVOLIO: I marvel your ladyship takes delight in such a barren rascal.

Viola, as Cesario, went to Lady Olivia's house. Malvolio tried to send her away. No matter what reason he gave for not letting her in, Viola had an answer. Lady Olivia decided to see this young man who would not go away. She put a veil[1] over her face.

Viola said that she wanted to speak to Lady Olivia alone. First, Olivia sent away her servants. Next, she took off her veil.

Olivia was very beautiful. Viola told her it was a pity to be so beautiful and not have any children while she was young. Viola spoke about her ideas of love. For the first time in many months, Olivia forgot her unhappiness and enjoyed talking to Viola.

Viola left. Suddenly, Olivia wanted to see "Cesario" again. She asked Malvolio to go after him and give him a ring. She pretended that Cesario had left the ring by mistake. Really, the ring was an excuse. She wanted to see Cesario again. She didn't know that Cesario was really Viola. She didn't know she was falling in love with a woman.

[1]veil – a covering, usually very thin, over the face

OLIVIA: Get you to your lord.
I cannot love him. Let him send no more –
Unless, perchance, you come to me again
To tell me how he takes it.

ACT TWO

Sebastian and his friend, Antonio, were talking together. Sebastian and his twin sister had been in a shipwreck. His sister had drowned, but Antonio had saved Sebastian.

Sebastian was going to Count Orsino's court[1]. Antonio had enemies there, because of things he had done in the past. He liked Sebastian. He decided to follow Sebastian, even though he knew he would be in danger.

[1]court – a rich person had a big house with many people living there. This was called a court.

SEBASTIAN: My father was that Sebastian of Messaline whom I know you have heard of. He left behind him myself and a sister, both born in an hour – if the heavens had been pleased, would we had so ended! But you, sir, altered that, for some hour before you took me from the breach of the sea was my sister drowned.

Malvolio followed Viola after she left Olivia's house. He gave her the ring, saying that Olivia was giving it back to her. Viola had not given Olivia a ring. This was puzzling. What did it mean? Olivia was behaving strangely. Was she falling in love with Cesario? That would be very complicated, because of course she, Viola, disguised as Cesario, was really a woman.

VIOLA: I left no ring with her; what means this lady?
Fortune forbid my outside have not charmed her!

Sir Toby Belch and Sir Andrew Aguecheek were drinking again. It was late in the evening. Feste, the clown, came in and they asked him to sing for them. He sang a love song.

They then began to get very noisy. They sang loudly together.

Maria told them to be quiet. They would get into trouble for making so much noise late at night.

MARIA: What a caterwauling do you keep here! If my lady have not called up her steward Malvolio and bid him turn you out of doors, never trust me.

Malvolio brought a message from Lady Olivia. If Sir Toby and his friends could not be quiet, they could leave her house. Malvolio behaved as if he was very important.

Sir Toby, who was drunk, did not take any notice. He and Feste kept on singing and made fun of Malvolio. Malvolio became furious and went to tell Lady Olivia.

Sir Toby, Sir Andrew and Maria thought Malvolio had behaved badly towards them.

Maria had a plan to get even with Malvolio. She and Lady Olivia had the same handwriting. Maria planned to write letters to Malvolio, as if they came from Lady Olivia. Maria's letters would make Malvolio think Lady Olivia was in love with him.

Maria, Sir Toby and Sir Andrew thought that would be great fun. They would make Malvolio look very silly. Sir Toby went off to have another drink.

MALVOLIO: My masters, are you mad? Or what are you? Have you no wit, manners, nor … honesty, but to gabble like tinkers at this time of night? Do ye make an alehouse of my lady's house…? Is there no respect of place, persons, nor time in you?

Viola and Orsino were listening to music. Orsino sent for Feste. He wanted to hear him sing a favourite song.

Orsino asked Viola if she had ever been in love, and with what kind of woman. Viola said that the person she loved looked like the Duke and was about the same age. This was the truth, because she loved the Duke.

Feste came and sang for the Duke. He sang a very sad song about love.

Orsino told Viola to go to see Olivia again. She was to take a precious jewel[1] and say that Orsino couldn't wait any longer for Olivia to love him.

[1]precious jewel – a piece of jewellery worth a lot of money

FESTE: Come away, come away, death,
And in sad cypress let me be laid.
Fie away, fie away, breath!
I am slain by a fair cruel maid.

Sir Toby and Sir Andrew and their friend Signor Fabian all hated Malvolio. Malvolio had got Signor Fabian into trouble with Lady Olivia. He had got Sir Toby and Sir Andrew into trouble. They all had reasons to hate Malvolio.

Maria had written a letter to Malvolio in Olivia's handwriting. The letter was supposed to come from Lady Olivia.

Malvolio was coming. Maria put the letter where he would see it. Sir Toby, Sir Andrew and Signor Fabian hid in a tree. They wanted to see what would happen.

Malvolio was thinking aloud. He was planning how he would behave if he married Lady Olivia. Sir Toby and the others would have to be very polite to him. He would tell Sir Toby to stop drinking.

These ideas made Sir Toby, Signor Fabian and Sir Andrew even more angry with Malvolio.

MALVOLIO: Cousin Toby, my fortunes having cast me on your niece give me this prerogative of speech...
SIR TOBY: What, what!
MALVOLIO: You must amend your drunkenness.
SIR TOBY: Out, scab!

Malvolio saw the letter that Maria had written. He was sure it came from Lady Olivia. It was in her handwriting.

Maria had written the letter very cleverly.

First, it said that Malvolio should be pleased, because he was going to become more important.

Second, he should be more rude to people.

Third, he should wear yellow stockings and cross his laces around his legs.

Finally, when he was with the writer of the letter, he should smile all the time.

Malvolio was sure that Olivia was the writer of the letter. He would do all the things she asked.

Maria had been very clever. The things the letter told Malvolio to do, were things that would annoy Lady Olivia. She hated yellow; she hated crossed laces; and she wanted people around her to be sad.

MARIA: If you will then see the fruits of the sport, mark his first approach before my lady. He will come to her in yellow stockings, and 'tis a colour she abhors; and cross-gartered, a fashion she detests; and he will smile upon her, which will now be so unsuitable to her disposition..."

ACT THREE

Viola went to Olivia's house again. On the way, she met Feste. She was kind to Feste and gave him money. She understood that it was difficult to be a jester.

Again, she told Olivia how much Orsino loved her. Olivia didn't want to talk about Orsino. Olivia was falling in love with Cesario. She didn't know that Cesario was really Viola. She didn't know that she was falling in love with a woman.

Viola said that she would never love any woman. This was true, because she loved Orsino. Olivia said that Cesario could come back and try to change her mind about Orsino. Really, she wanted to see Cesario again.

OLIVIA: Cesario, by the roses of the spring,
By maidhood, honour, truth, and everything,
I love thee so that, maugre all thy pride,
Nor wit nor reason can my passion hide.

Sir Andrew saw Olivia and Viola talking. He could see that Olivia liked Cesario. Sir Toby told Sir Andrew that he needed to get Olivia's respect. Sir Andrew should fight Cesario. He should challenge him to a duel[1].

Sir Andrew went off to write his challenge.

Maria came in, laughing. Malvolio was following every point in her letter. He was walking about in yellow stockings, with his laces criss-crossed. He was smiling all the time.

They all went to have a look at Malvolio.

[1]challenge him to a duel – tell him he wanted a fight

SIR TOBY: Challenge me the Count's youth to fight with him; hurt him in eleven places; my niece shall take note of it... and, assure thyself, there is no love-broker in the world can more prevail in man's commendation with woman than report of valour.

In another part of the town, Antonio had caught up with Sebastian. They decided not to walk around the town together. Antonio had fought with some of the people there. He had enemies.

Antonio went to find a place to stay and to order some food. He gave Sebastian his purse in case he saw something to buy. They agreed to meet later.

Sebastian did not have much money of his own. It was very kind of Antonio to give him the purse. He went to look around the town.

SEBASTIAN: Why I your purse?
ANTONIO: Haply your eye shall light upon some toy
You have desire to purchase; and your store,
I think, is not for idle markets, sir.
SEBASTIAN: I'll be your purse-bearer, and leave you for
An hour.

Lady Olivia sent for Malvolio. Maria warned her that Malvolio was behaving strangely.

Malvolio was smiling and kissing his hand. He wore yellow stockings. Olivia hated yellow stockings. His laces were criss-crossed in the way Olivia hated.

Olivia wanted him to be serious, but he kept on smiling and kissing his hand.

He quoted[1] words from the letter Maria had written. None of it made any sense to Olivia.

Sir Toby, Fabian and Maria were very pleased. Malvolio was making a fool of himself. They planned more mischief for him. They were enjoying their joke.

[1]quoted – repeated exactly

OLIVIA: Smil'st thou? I sent for thee upon a sad occasion.

MALVOLIO: Sad, lady? I could be sad; this does make some obstruction in the blood, this cross-gartering – but what of that? If it please the eye of one, it is with me as the very true sonnet is: 'Please one and please all'.

Viola saw Lady Olivia again. Olivia asked her to wear a special small picture with jewels around it. It was a picture of Olivia. Olivia was now sure that she loved "Cesario". This was not at all what Viola wanted.

OLIVIA: Here, wear this jewel for me, 'tis my picture.
Refuse it not, it hath no tongue to vex you.
And, I beseech you, come again tomorrow.

Viola was leaving Olivia's house. Sir Toby told her that Sir Andrew was not looking for a fight. Viola did not want to fight. Also, she had not quarrelled with Sir Andrew.

Sir Toby came back with Sir Andrew. Sir Toby was telling lies about Viola. He said that Cesario was a clever fighter. He couldn't wait to fight Sir Andrew.

Sir Andrew was very frightened. He changed his mind about fighting. He said he would give Cesario a horse if he would call off the fight.

Instead of telling the truth, Sir Toby lied to Viola. He said that Sir Andrew still wanted to have a fight, but promised not to hurt Cesario.

He then lied yet again to Sir Andrew. He said Cesario still wanted to fight, but didn't want to hurt Sir Andrew.

In fact, Viola was so frightened, she was ready to tell them she was a woman, not a man.

VIOLA: *(aside)* Pray God defend me! A little thing would make me tell them how much I lack of a man.

Antonio saw the fighting. He thought that Viola was his friend, Sebastian. They looked alike. They were dressed in the same clothes. He tried to stop the fight.

Count Orsino's men came along. They recognised Antonio as a former enemy. They arrested him. Antonio asked Viola for his purse. Viola had no idea what he was talking about.

ANTONIO: This comes with seeking you.
But there's no remedy, I shall answer it.
What will you do, now my necessity
Makes me to ask you for my purse?

Viola could see that Antonio truly believed she was someone else. Also, he called her Sebastian. That was her brother's name.

Was it possible that her brother was alive? She had dressed like her brother and tried to be like him in every way. She began to think that her brother might have escaped the storm after all.

VIOLA: Methinks his words do from such passion fly
That he believes himself; so do not I?
Prove true, imagination, O, prove true –
That I, dear brother, be now ta'en for you!

ACT FOUR

Feste met Sebastian. He thought he was talking to Orsino's servant Cesario.

Sir Andrew came along and hit Sebastian, thinking he was hitting Cesario. Sebastian hit back. He hit very hard. He was not afraid to fight.

Feste went to fetch Lady Olivia. She would not want Cesario to be in a fight.

Lady Olivia arrived just as Sir Toby was about to join in.

SIR ANDREW:	Now, sir, have I met you again? There's for you!
	(he strikes Sebastian)
SEBASTIAN:	Why, there's for thee! And there! And there! Are all the people mad?

Lady Olivia did not want any fighting. She sent Sir Toby and the others away.

Of course, she also thought that Sebastian was Cesario, whom she loved.

She invited Sebastian to her house, and spoke to him in a loving way. Sebastian could not believe his good luck.

SEBASTIAN: What relish is in this? How runs the stream?
Or I am mad, or else this is a dream.
Let fancy still my sense in Lethe steep;
If it be thus to dream, still let me sleep!

Maria and Sir Toby shut Malvolio in a dark cellar. They were telling him he was mad.

Feste pretended to be Sir Topas, a curate[1]. Malvolio said he was in a dark prison. Feste told him it was not dark. It was beautiful and full of light.

They were all trying to send Malvolio crazy. Sir Toby was getting tired of the joke.

Feste had some fun pretending to be two people. He spoke and sang in his own voice, then as Sir Topas, the curate.

In the end, Feste helped poor Malvolio. He went to fetch a light, paper and ink, so that Malvolio could write to Olivia.

[1]curate – a man from the church

MALVOLIO: I am not mad, Sir Topas. I say to you, this house is dark.
FESTE: Madman, thou errest. I say there is no darkness but ignorance…

Sebastian had fallen in love with Lady Olivia. She was in love with him, even though she still thought that he was Cesario (who was really Viola!).

She asked Sebastian to go with her and a priest to the church. They would promise to be married.

Sebastian agreed to the promise, and said he would always be true to Olivia. He didn't know that she thought he was Cesario.

SEBASTIAN: I'll follow this good man, and go with you;
And having sworn truth, ever will be true.

ACT FIVE

Orsino and Viola were going to see Lady Olivia. They met the officers with the captured Antonio.

Viola said that Antonio had saved her from a fight. The officers reminded Orsino that Antonio had caused him a lot of trouble. Orsino asked Antonio why he had come back to a place where he had so many enemies.

Antonio was very angry. He thought that Viola was Sebastian. He said that he had saved him from the sea. They had been together for three months, and had become friends. He followed his friend to the town to protect him.

Three months: Viola was saved from the sea three months before. She had been Orsino's servant for three months.

ANTONIO: That most ungrateful boy there by your side
From the rude sea's enraged and foamy mouth
Did I redeem; a wrack past hope he was,
His life I gave him, and did thereto add
My love without retention or restraint,
All his in dedication.

Olivia came in. Olivia was angry. She thought that "Cesario" had just promised, in the church, to marry her. She reminded Cesario of the promise.

Orsino was very angry too. Viola was supposed to make Olivia love him. Instead, Olivia had fallen in love with Cesario.

Olivia called Cesario her husband, and asked the priest to tell about the promises they had made.

Orsino was more angry than ever. He wouldn't listen to Viola, who knew that she hadn't made any promises to marry anyone. He said he would have nothing more to do with Cesario.

No one knew about Sebastian. He truly loved Olivia and had promised to marry her.

ORSINO: Farewell, and take her; but direct thy feet
Where you and I henceforth may never meet.
VIOLA: My lord, I do protest —

Sir Andrew was holding his head. He and Sir Toby thought they had been fighting with Cesario. In fact, they had been fighting with Sebastian, who was very strong. They both had bloody heads.

OLIVIA: Who has done this, Sir Andrew?
SIR ANDREW: The Count's gentleman, one Cesario. We took him for a coward, but he's the very devil incarnate.

Sebastian came to apologise to Olivia for hurting her uncle, Sir Toby.

For the first time, everyone saw Viola and Sebastian together.

They looked alike. Viola was still dressed as a boy. Sebastian had never had a brother, only a sister. If she had been a woman, she could have been the sister he thought drowned. What a shame she was a boy!

Viola started to talk about her family. Her father was Sebastian of Messaline. That was the name of Sebastian's father.

Viola's father had a mole[1] on his forehead. Sebastian's father had a mole, too.

Viola's father had died on her thirteenth birthday. Sebastian's had too!

Viola at last told them all that she was really a woman, and would go and put on her woman's clothes. She was indeed Viola, Sebastian's sister.

[1]mole – large brown pimple

SEBASTIAN: Were you a woman, as the rest goes even,
I should my tears let fall upon your cheek,
And say, "Thrice welcome, drowned Viola."

Now, Olivia knew that she had promised to marry Sebastian. She loved Sebastian, even though she had thought he was Cesario at the time!

Orsino realised that he was falling in love with Viola. He had liked his servant Cesario because he could share all his thoughts. Now, he wanted to see Cesario dressed as a woman: a woman he could love.

Olivia remembered Malvolio. She had him brought to her. He showed the letter that Maria had written, pretending to be Olivia. Olivia told him it was not her writing. Maria had written it.

It was all part of the trick against Malvolio. Fabian and Feste reminded Malvolio that he had been rude to all of them. That was why they had planned the tricks.

Malvolio was still angry. He went away saying he would get revenge[1].

Olivia felt sorry for him.

[1]revenge – getting one's own back

OLIVIA: Alas, Malvolio, this is not my writing,
Though, I confess, much like the character.
But out of question 'tis Maria's hand.,

At the end of the story, there were three happy couples. Sir Toby had married Maria. Olivia and Sebastian were betrothed[1].

Orsino was quite sure he would love Viola when at last he saw her in her woman's clothes.

They all went off to make their plans.

Feste sang a farewell song: a song to remind everyone that life was not always easy; a song to say that the actors in the play had worked hard. The play was done.

[1]betrothed – had promised to be married

FESTE: A great while ago the world began,
With hey-ho, the wind and the rain;
But that's all one, our play is done,
And we'll strive to please you every day.